BEAUTY, BRAVE AND BEAUTIFUL

BEAUTY, BRAVE AND BEAUTIFUL

by Dick Gackenbach

Clarion Books

New York

Watercolors and a sepia pen line
were used to create the full-color art.
The text type is 14 pt. Jensen.

Clarion Books
a Houghton Mifflin Company imprint
215 Park Avenue South, New York, NY 10003
Text and Illustrations copyright © 1990 by Dick Gackenbach

Library of Congress Cataloging-in-Publication Data
Gackenbach, Dick.
Beauty, brave and beautiful / Dick Gackenbach.
p. cm.
Summary: A surprising event occurs after the townsfolk build a
statue to honor a homeless dog they believe died in a struggle to
save two children from a bear.
ISBN 0-395-52000-2
1. Dogs—Juvenile fiction.   [1. Dogs—Fiction.]   I. Title.
PZ10.3.G116Be   1990
89-17418
[E]—dc20   CIP
                          AC

WOZ 10 9 8 7 6 5 4 3 2 1

FOR CHUCK AND BOB

I

A long time ago, in a litter with three cute and cuddly pups, a sorry-looking pup was born. She was the runt of the litter. Her eyes were crossed, one eye green, the other brown. Her legs were crooked and her tail was bent. Her nose looked like a tomato, and her fur was as coarse as winter grass.

When it was time to leave their mother, the three cute pups quickly found a home, but the ugly pup had no such luck. When she scratched on farmhouse doors, hoping for hugs and kisses and warm words of welcome, she was greeted with, "Shoo! Shoo!" and "Away with you. There's no room for you here!"

Even worse than the harsh words was the sting of a broom on her tail.

After a while she lost the courage to go near a door again for fear of being struck. Dazed and frightened, the little pup went off to the woods to live by herself. In the woods, she grew into a young dog with a sweet and gentle nature. But unfortunately, she grew no prettier than she had been as a pup.

Life in the woods was not too bad for the dog. There were berries to gobble and tasty roots to nibble on, and an occasional field mouse for dinner. There was always fresh water to drink, and warm hollow tree stumps to keep her snug and warm on wintry nights. But it was not a happy life for the little dog. She longed to be patted on the head and scratched behind the ears. Although she didn't know it, the dog wished for human company.

Early one summer morning, the dog's wish came true. She was chasing a fat field mouse into a clearing when she saw a boy and girl playing. The boy was named Jacob, and the girl was his little sister, Kate.

At first, the dog was very cautious. She got down on her belly and hid in the tall grass while she watched the children play. Now and then she shoved her big nose up from her hiding place to sniff. The children had a fine, friendly smell about them.

The dog watched the children run and climb trees. They were having so much fun that every muscle in the dog's body began to twitch. She longed to join them.

When she was certain the children did not have a broom with them, the dog could stand it no longer. She barked a loud greeting. Then her tail wagged and her rear end shook as she jumped from her hiding place.

"Look, Jacob!" cried Kate. "Do you think it's friendly?"

"What a funny-looking dog," said Jacob. "But it seems friendly. See! Its tail is wagging."

The children ran across the clearing to meet the dog. When they got near, they held their hands out for the dog to sniff.

"It's a girl," remarked Jacob.

"Nice doggy," said Kate. "Do you think she wants something to eat?" she asked her brother.

"I don't think it's food she wants," said Jacob as he looked into the dog's odd little face. "I think she wants someone to play with her." Jacob picked up a stick and tossed it. "Fetch!" he yelled.

The dog ran after the stick and, tail wagging, brought it back to Jacob's feet.

"Good girl," praised Jacob as he patted the dog on the head. The little dog whimpered. At that moment she was as happy as she had ever been.

The children stayed in the clearing and played with the dog all day. They romped and raced together in the fields and by the stream. They played hide-and-seek behind the rocks and trees. And Jacob threw the stick so many times the little dog became breathless. The children even shared their lunch with the dog, so there was no need for her to stop the fun and search for a fat mouse.

When the day was over, Jacob and Kate tried their best to take the dog home with them, but she would not leave the woods. Although she trusted the children, the dog still had no use for the town. She had been chased and shooed away by the broom too many times.

After Jacob and Kate had gone, the dog felt lonely and friendless again. She curled up in an old tree stump, but she could not sleep. Lying there, she thought about the glorious day and her new friends. Would they return and play with her tomorrow, she wondered?

II

At dawn the next morning, even before the birds began to chirp in the trees, the little dog went to the clearing. She waited for Kate and Jacob with that patience only dogs possess when waiting for a human friend.

The dog was not disappointed, for Jacob and Kate did return to look for her. They came back the next day, and the next, and every day after that. And each day Jacob and Kate brought something special for the dog. Some of the gifts were useful, like a bone or tasty table scraps. Some were not so useful, like a brass-studded red collar which the dog wore only to please the children.

One day, Kate told Jacob, "We can't go on calling her 'dog'. She should have a proper name."

"I agree," said Jacob. "Let's think of one."

"Well," said Kate, "there's Sarah, Charlotte, Agnes, Emily, Annabelle, Bebe, Clara, Zenobia, Tessie, or Daphne."

Jacob shook his head. "None of those seem to fit," he said. "How about Plucky, Bandit, Vagabond, Jiffy, Spunky, Skipper, or Smacker?"

"No, no!" insisted Kate. "I don't care for those. It must be a name that's just right."

So the children sat down and took a good hard look at their friend. The dog perked up her ears and tried her best to understand what the children were doing. Why didn't they throw the stick? she wondered. She put her head down on her paws and started to take a nap. Just when she was about to go to sleep, she heard the little girl give a shout.

"I've got it!" said Kate. "I've got the perfect name!"

She grabbed her brother's hand. "Don't you think she's beautiful?" she asked.

Jacob studied the dog carefully. He looked her over from head to tail and could see no imperfections. All Jacob saw was an animal he loved very much.

"Yes, she's beautiful," he said. "So what's the perfect name?"

"Beauty," replied Kate proudly.

Jacob smiled. "I like it," he said. Then he turned to the dog. "What do you think of that, girl? Beauty! Beauty! Beauty!" Each time Jacob said the name he tapped Beauty on her head to let her know it belonged to her.

Then Jacob took up a stick and spelled out the name in the dirt. B-E-A-U-T-Y, he wrote. Beauty watched as the boy wrote each letter. When he was done, she pounced on him with her hairy paws and barked.

"Do you think she knows her name?" asked Kate.

"Yes," said Jacob. "But now I think she's telling us she wants to play." Jacob threw the stick, and Beauty brought it back. "Good dog," Jacob said. "Good Beauty."

Over the summer days that followed, Jacob and Kate taught Beauty many tricks.

"Sit," said Jacob. And Beauty sat.

"Play dead," commanded Kate. And Beauty rolled over and put her paws in the air.

"Come, Beauty," they called, and Beauty came.

Those were happy days for the dog. And the nights were good, too, for she dreamed of the children. Beauty was no longer lonely, and even the fear of the broom was starting to fade.

A peaceful summer passed and turned into a lazy fall. One day in late September, Jacob was reading a book aloud and Beauty was dozing with her head on Kate's lap.

Suddenly the branches of a large hemlock trembled, and a great bear appeared from behind the tree. The bear roared to announce his presence. Then his small, mean eyes narrowed, and his nose and lips curled back slowly to show his pointed yellow teeth.

III

At first sight of the savage creature, Beauty jumped up and placed herself between the children and the ferocious bear. Jacob dropped his book and grabbed Kate by the hand. The two children ran for help while Beauty stood her ground.

When the bear made a move to follow Kate and Jacob, Beauty sank her teeth into the animal's hind leg and hung on for dear life. The enraged beast sent down a shower of blows on Beauty. His long, sharp claws tore at the little dog, but she would not let go.

Roars, snarls, and growls echoed through the woods and frightened the birds away. The sound of snapping jaws rang out like firecrackers over the ponds, sending tiny frogs beneath the lily pads. Then, as suddenly as it began, the battle ended and an eerie quiet filled the woods.

Soon the silence was broken by the sounds of running feet and the cries of children. "Beauty, Beauty," called Kate. "We're coming," shouted Jacob.

The children had returned with their father. He charged into the clearing, his gun loaded and ready, but he could see no animal to aim at. The bear was gone and so, it seemed, was Beauty.

"Where is Beauty?" Kate sobbed. "We must find her. She may be in terrible trouble."

The three began to search for the dog. Kate looked by the rocks and the fiddlehead ferns. Jacob pushed through the brambles and the skunk cabbage. Their father looked beneath the tangled branches of underbrush. "Beauty! Beauty!" the three of them called as they searched. But all they found amid the signs of hard fighting were bits of ragged fur.

During the weeks that followed, the children and their father returned to the woods every day to look for the missing dog. Along the way, Kate and Jacob told their father all about their love for the sweet and gentle Beauty. They told him about the games they had played, and the tricks they had taught her.

On the day of the first winter snow, Jacob caught sight of something red. "Look here," he shouted as he picked up Beauty's red, brass-studded collar from the new-fallen snow.

"Well, that seems to settle it," said their father. "The bear must have carried her off." Kate's eyes filled with tears. Jacob put his arm around his sister, and their father tried to comfort them both.

"Beauty was a faithful friend," he reminded them.

"She was a wonderful dog," said Jacob.

"And she saved our lives," Kate said sadly.

"I know," replied the father. "And for that I shall always be grateful."

He knelt down and looked first at Kate and then at Jacob. "I told the Mayor and the Town Council about Beauty and her bravery," he said. "And they have decided to build a monument to honor her."

"How wonderful!" Kate said, and clapped her hands.

"Now Beauty will never be forgotten," said Jacob.

A few days after that, their father took Jacob and Kate to see a sculptor.

"Now tell me," said the artist, "what this Beauty looked like so that I can create an image of her."

"Well," Kate began, "Beauty had a long, pointed nose, and her legs were straight and fast as arrows."

"And," added Jacob, "her fur was soft as silk—with a curly, bushy tail."

"And she had the most beautiful eyes you've ever seen," they both agreed.

While the cold months of winter passed, the artist worked with hammer and chisel, shaping the statue according to Kate's and Jacob's description.

When the model was finished, the artist made a mold of it. He filled the mold with melted copper, tin, lead and zinc, and when the metals hardened, they were bronze. Then the artist covered the bronze with gold.

The gold statue was placed on a marble base with an inscription that read simply: BEAUTY, BRAVE AND BEAUTIFUL.

In the spring, the golden statue was unveiled on the square in the center of town.

The Mayor was there. All the members of the Town Council were there. And Kate and Jacob were the guests of honor.

"Well, what do you think?" the Mayor asked the children when he pulled the sheet away from the statue.

Kate was thrilled. "It's magnificent," she said. "It looks just like our Beauty."

"The spitting image," said Jacob.

Everyone who saw it had to agree with Kate and Jacob that Beauty was a most beautiful dog indeed.

"But isn't it a pity," they said, "that she was eaten by a bear."

BEAUTY,
BRAVE
AND
BEAUTIFUL

IV

That wasn't what really happened, though. Everyone believed Beauty had ended up in the belly of the bear, but she had not.

When Beauty knew the children were safely out of harm's way, she had released her fangs from the bear's leg. She knew she was no match for such a vicious beast. Remembering the trick Kate had taught her, Beauty dropped to the ground and played dead.

The bear sniffed around the dog as she lay still with her legs in the air. Not much of a meal, he thought. So, after giving Beauty one last swipe with his great paw, the bear crept back into the woods in search of other mischief.

When Beauty was certain the bear had gone, she managed to crawl away from the clearing. She crawled for a long time until she found a safe and hidden tree stump. There she spent the cold winter months, catching an occasional field mouse for dinner and licking her many wounds.

By spring, Beauty was still a pitiful sight. The vision in her brown eye was gone, and she had lost half her tail and the tip of one ear in the fight. Patches of fur were missing and she walked with a limp. But her spirits were high, and her nature was as sweet as ever.

In April, the birds returned to the trees and the frogs were singing again in the ponds. The warm spring breezes made Beauty think of Kate and Jacob. Now that she was well, she longed to be with the two of them again. But how would she find them?

She thought of the clearing—perhaps they'd be there! With the stump of her tail wagging, Beauty made her way back over brooks and ditches to the edge of the woods. At the clearing, the little dog waited day after day, but the children did not come.

Had the children forgotten her? No, Beauty was certain that they had loved her as much as she loved them. There was only one thing to do. If she was going to find the children again, she would have to leave the woods. Beauty's heart pounded at the thought of the brooms. Despite her fears, she gathered all her courage and slowly limped toward town.

Beauty began to tremble when she reached the first house. Cautiously, she stayed close by the walls and fences with her head down and her tail between her legs. At last, happy that no one had seen her, she reached the town square.

While she rested and wondered how to cross such a wide-open space without being seen, her good eye saw the great golden statue. She could hardly believe it, a statue of a dog! Forgetting her fears, Beauty trotted out into the square to have a closer look at the statue. It was the most perfect dog she had ever seen. Not like me, she thought.

Then Beauty saw her name. There it was, the very name Kate had given her and Jacob had spelled out in the dirt. B-E-A-U-T-Y! The dog fixed her eye on the letters and stared.

After a while, people passing by noticed the odd little dog sitting in front of the magnificent statue. It was quite a sight. Some of them pointed at Beauty and laughed.

"Look at that ridiculous dog," said one.

"Don't you wish you looked like that statue?" said another.

"That's what I call an ugly dog," snickered a third.

A bully tried to shoo Beauty away, but the dog would not budge. Listen to me, I am Beauty, she wanted to say. But, of course, she could not.

Soon word of the dog spread and a crowd gathered. People came out of their houses, the library, and shops. Even the school was let out so the children could see what all the commotion was about.

Kate and Jacob arrived at the square with their classmates. When Beauty saw Kate and Jacob, she barked and ran in circles. When the children saw Beauty, they jumped up and down, exploding with joy.

"It's a miracle," cried Kate.

"It's our Beauty," shouted Jacob to the crowd. "She's alive!"

What a reunion they had! It seemed the hugs and kisses, the tail wagging and the barking would go on forever.

When things calmed down, and people realized this was the dog who had saved Kate and Jacob, some of them wanted to cart the statue away. "The dog doesn't look like the statue at all," they said.

But when they thought it over, they changed their minds. "She may not be a beauty," they decided at last, "but you can't deny her bravery."

So the statue remained, and so did Beauty. She went to live with Kate and Jacob. At night, she slept at the foot of Kate's bed. But she liked to spend her days sitting proudly at the base of her statue.

Folks began to go out of their way to stop and pet the little dog, and in time her fur began to feel as soft to them as silk.

People stopped and scratched her ears, and soon her legs did not look crooked, nor the stub of her tail so bent.

They looked deep into her one good eye and saw the sweetness there. "What a beautiful dog," they said.

As the town began to love her, they no longer noticed any difference at all between the little dog and the noble statue.

And from that time on, if a cross-eyed, sorry-looking pup happened to scratch at someone's door, it was never shooed away. Instead it was welcomed, and given a happy home.